Christy Ann C

Dead Time

Isabella wants to scream. She didn't do anything!

The youth workers tell Isabella she needs to work on her attitude, but who the hell do they think they are?

Isabella's serving "dead time" in a detention center until she's tried for the killing of Sergei's ex-girlfriend, Lulu.

Lulu walked into the store that day in January and winked at Sergei, all sexy and coy. Of course Isabella was jealous, not that she'd admit it to Sergei. That was just the beginning of the whole trouble.

Prove you love me, Sergei, she said. How could she know he'd lose control?

Now she waits for Sergei to do the right thing and tell them the truth, that it's his fault. *Or else.*

Single Voice

1 book | 2 stories

Also available in the Single Voice series

**FILM STUDIES
| THE TROUBLE WITH MARLENE**
Caroline Adderson | Billie Livingston

"Teens who love gritty, real life stories with "what if?" situations are sure to like these stories."
—CM Magazine

Two startling stories about the powerful impact of parents' behavior on teens

In *Film Studies*, Cass's movie director father is sophisticated, always traveling. Cass wonders what role she should play. Along comes a new guy and a school film project—and things get strange.

Samantha's mother Marlene spends her days drinking and imagining the perfect suicide. No one has any idea what Sammie's world is like, except Drew, and she's not sure she wants to let him in. In *The Trouble with Marlene*, Sammie wonders what's so great about this life, anyway?

Single Voice

Christy Ann Conlin

Dead Time

annick press
toronto + new york + vancouver

Annick Press Ltd.

Series editor: Melanie Little

Copyedited by Pam Robertson
Cover design by David Drummond/Salamander Hill Design
Cover photo (keys) by STILLFX / shutterstock.com
Interior design by Monica Charny

We acknowledge the support of the Canada Council for the Arts, the Ontario Arts Council, and the Government of Canada through the Canada Book Fund (CBF) for our publishing activities.

 **ONTARIO ARTS COUNCIL**
CONSEIL DES ARTS DE L'ONTARIO

Cataloging in Publication

Conlin, Christy Ann
        Dead time / Christy Ann Conlin.

(Single voice series)
Title on added t.p., inverted: Shelter / Jen Sookfong Lee.
ISBN 978-1-55451-287-4 (bound).—ISBN 978-1-55451-286-7 (pbk.)

        I. Lee, Jen Sookfong II. Title. III. Series: Single voice (Toronto, Ont.)

PS8555.O5378D42 2011   jC813'.6   C2010-907286-3

Published in the U.S.A. by
Annick Press (U.S.) Ltd.

Distributed in Canada by
Firefly Books Ltd.
66 Leek Crescent
Richmond Hill, ON
L4B 1H1

Distributed in the U.S.A. by
Firefly Books (U.S.) Inc.
P.O. Box 1338
Ellicott Station
Buffalo, NY 14205

Visit our website at www.annickpress.com
Visit Christy Ann Conlin at www.christyannconlin.com

Guilty, guilty, guilty, their eyes all say,
the words scratching themselves into the
concrete walls. Beige. It's the color of the
whole penal institution, which is what it
is even though they call it a youth center,
like it's a community club—a locked club
with bars on the windows.

But I'm telling you, I'm not. There was
nothing I could do once Sergei started. He
would have killed me. He was in a rage

and all I could do was scream. I tried to stop him, but how can you stop someone who's obsessed?

That's what the youth worker accused me of when I got here. Being *obsessed* with myself. Can you believe it? We were in the dining hall and I said I wasn't going to eat the dried-out mashed potatoes from a box.

"The food sucks in here," I said in a loud voice. Well, didn't that fat youth worker at the end of the table tell me to be quiet. I was so pissed off.

"Be quiet? Is that what you said to me?" I yelled when she came over to where I was

sitting. "You can't tell me what to do."
She was standing right over me. And she
laughed. I couldn't believe it. Like I was a
big joke. *No one* laughs at me.

"Yes, Isabella, I *can* tell you what to do.
And I'll tell you that you should stop
obsessing over yourself and what you want
and think about other people for a change.
Maybe the girl who died. The girl they
say you killed. Maybe think about her for
once."

Her. Lulu. Like I wanted to think about *her*.

It was Lulu, Sergei's stupid ex, who caused all these horrible problems in the first place, starting the day we saw her at the store. Lulu didn't go the same school as us and I'd never really thought much about her until that day in January, when we were buying popsicles. She was tiny, with long hair and a ruby red nose stud. "Hi Sergei," she said in this cutesy voice, looking down at her feet and then looking up. She didn't even wait for him to say hello, just walked out. And right before she did she winked at him, right in front of me, a sexy wink with her long eyelashes, all coy.

What nerve. Winking was *our* thing. That

was how we got together. I'm the one who winks at Sergei, not *her*. Winking was supposed to be our special bond. She's not winking these days, now is she.

I was watching him all the time after that. Sergei denied it, said she didn't wink. Like he thought I was blind. How insulting. It was so obvious. He said Lulu was really shy, she wouldn't do that kind of thing. I didn't talk to him all the way home, and when he parked the car in my driveway he told me not to be jealous. I wanted to stick a fork in him when he said that. Of course I was jealous—but I wasn't going to let him know that. Who did he think he was to accuse *me* of being jealous of *her*?

I made myself laugh, like I didn't care. "Why would I be jealous? *You* dumped her," I said with my eyes almost closed.

His hands got tight on the steering wheel and the yellow skin on the side of his index finger from all the weed he smokes was so bright against the black vinyl. "So?" he said.

Lulu. Who did she think she was that she could just wink and come on to my boyfriend like that? Like I was invisible, like I was some stand-in for her.

━━ •

The fat youth worker just stood there, looking down at me, like she thought I was going to suddenly say I was guilty or something. I could feel my heart going boom-banga, boom-boom and then I just lost it. I stood up and threw my mashed potatoes right in her pudgy face, plate and all. Well, they came from everywhere, the youth workers, throwing me to the floor, arms behind my back, and then they carried me like I was an Egyptian mummy into my cell. They took out everything and left me there on the concrete floor. Bastards. I was so mad. It was humiliating. They sent in the senior supervisor for the night and he told me I was lucky the youth worker wasn't going to charge me with assault.

"For throwing a plastic plate of mashed potatoes?" I said to him. I rolled my eyes. "Come on. It's not like she didn't deserve it."

"You can't even see how that is wrong, can you?" He looked like he was feeling sorry for me, but not because I was trapped in here, but like he thought I was some heartless freak. His pager went off and then he left, but not before looking at me and shaking his head. I'd like to give him a shake.

I hate them all. They keep telling me I

need to work on my attitude, honesty
is important, taking responsibility is
important, like they think I'm a liar. I have
no problem telling them where they can
shove their comments because who the
hell are they to talk down to me?

▬▬▬ ●

It's been three months I've been sitting in
here. It took three weeks for my throat to
stop aching from screaming at Sergei. *Just
let her go.* He didn't have to prove anything
to me. He turned on me then. The bruises
on my face have faded now. At first they
turned green and red and purple as though
I'd rubbed my cheek on some strange

plant in a pond deep in a forest, some
magic pond. Bad magic. In fairy tales
girls like me turn the magic around. The
heroines always take control.

I press my lips together, lips that would
feel better with lipstick but there is no
lipstick in this place. No nail polish. It's
all about pale here, washed-out walls, dull
boring carpets. Boring colors that don't
tell you anything. You can't trust beige.

It will take a long time to move past all
of this, everything that has happened,
the way they are treating me in here. My
father says I will need a lot of counseling.
He says the police say I did it but my

lawyer is going to demand that I be released once they give Sergei's statement to the court, saying that he was the one. My lawyer's going to tell the judge I have post-traumatic stress disorder. PTSD from watching Sergei murder that girl. PTSD. It sounds like the name of a band.

The warden is old, almost fifty, I bet, older than my dad. There is no kindness in his blue eyes. There's something else in there but I haven't figured out what it is yet. I will. But he's got a shield up. He's seen it all, he tells me.

They act like everyone in here is guilty, even me, on remand, with no trial yet.

The warden says he knows I'm afraid, it's normal, but I need to show respect. I can't yell at the staff. I can't throw things. He says it doesn't matter how angry I get, how upset, there are appropriate ways to behave and I'll be in here for a lot longer if I don't behave.

"Even if they're rude to *me?*" I ask him. "If they don't show *me* respect?"

"Expecting you to do what they say, when they say it, isn't rude," he says.

"You don't know what's it's like to be locked up."

"No," he says, "I don't. You should have thought of that before."

"But I didn't do anything," I tell him.

He nods. "Yes, so you say."

I won't give him the satisfaction of a reply
this time. I just look away. He doesn't
care that I'm really a victim too. He thinks
because my father is a politician I feel
entitled to special treatment. I don't.

"They'll be here for you soon," he says. He
leaves and I look at the door as he walks out.

Click.

That sharp sound of the door locking
fills the cell and then fades into a dream
sound, muffled and faraway echoing.

Click, click.

My mother used to tap her shoe when she wanted something done. She'll have been gone for three years in the spring and I can still hear the click her high heels made on the ceramic tile.

Click when the door closed behind her. The click the phone made when she'd hang up during our Sunday call after she left and moved. She always said she had to hang up before I was ready to stop talking. And then I would hear the sound of the call ending.

Clickity, clack, I'm not coming back.

"It's not you," she said, that first call. "It's me." Like she was breaking up with me. "I just can't pass up the opportunity to live in a house on the beach with palm trees. And be with someone who's home more often than not." And someone half her age— she didn't mention that.

Snap. My father flipping his phone shut.

Snap, snap, snicky snap. We don't need her, shut her trap.

"You're old enough to be left alone," he said the next morning, "twelve years old is more than old enough. We'll manage. Let her have her palm trees."

And then he was off to work, before I was even dressed to go out and wait for the school bus.

Beep. His car started with a flick of his button.

The garage door opened with another click. Off he drove.

And click as I shut the door to the house.

The walls of our house were beige then. Sable, my mother had called them. Sable, she would say, picking up a crystal hour-glass she had, *tawny, sandy, sandy dune, sparkling in the sun of June,* turning it upside down on the table by the window

where the afternoon sun streamed in,
watching every grain drift down.

It's hard to keep track of time in here.
Every day is the same. I've been to court
three times already. They cuff me and
shackle me. Strip-search me when I come
back. Like I'm a common criminal. My
hands keep sweating. I don't know why. I
mean, I'm not nervous or anything. Sergei
said he'd tell them and I know they'll drop
the charges. I don't know why it's taking
them so long to check out his story.

I told him, when we were waiting there
by the pond for the police to come, if he
didn't say it, if he tried to blame me, I
would tell them where his grow op was,
his big marijuana patch, they'd take his
house away and then his grandmother, the
old wrinkled babushka that he worships,
would have nowhere to live and they'd
stick her in a home. They always confiscate
drug property, don't they? I said I'd tell
them he forced me to have sex with him
even though that's not true. I told him
if he really loved me, if he wanted to
prove his love, then he would be a man
and say he did it, that true love is about
proving your love. I mean, he has to take
responsibility and I'm not beyond forcing

him to do that. I told it all to the police,
what happened to his ex-girlfriend. They
went over and over the story with me, and
I told them the same thing every time.
You didn't help him? they asked. You
didn't drown her? I started to cry then.
That they would think I could do that. She
fell in the pond. I couldn't reach her. It
was too deep.

This whole thing is her fault, Sergei's fault.
When we started seeing each other he
never talked about her—I never knew a
thing about her until that day we were at
the store getting popsicles and cigarettes
and she was at the cash paying. She looked
up and smiled, at him, not me. That's
when the trouble started.

And I know Sergei will do the right thing. *Or else*, I told him. He made all of this happen. I keep going over and over what happened because it's easy to get the story mixed up. It's like it's a comic book. I can see it in my mind whether my eyes are open or shut. It was so confusing at first, trying to remember, because it happened so fast. But then I remembered, piece by piece, picture by picture. I told the police how Sergei just went crazy. That he was fanatical when it came to proving his love for me, that he was fixated on getting rid of her. I wanted to help her but I was scared of doing anything because he was so out of control. I realized he was crazy and maybe it could have been me lying in the lily pond, not her. Just a snap of the fingers and our roles reversed. "I wish it *was* me," I told my father and the police. "I wish it was me and not her who had to suffer," I said with my voice cracking. I couldn't believe how upset I sounded. My father's eyes filled up with tears and he said in a very kind voice that I wasn't responsible for Sergei and what he did, that I shouldn't blame myself.

▬▬ ●

Being locked up is probably harder on other kids in here than it is on me. I'm used to being on my own because my father is always working. But I'm also used to doing what I want and that's what's hard in here. I can't piss unless they authorize it. When I first realized they were going to charge me, I lost it. I was screaming and crying and this youth worker did what they call "non-violent crisis intervention." Those words, "youth worker"—what a joke. She's a guard; they should just be honest about that. I'm a prisoner. It's a prison. I don't know why they have to make up all this language to hide the truth. Who do they think they are fooling?

There's a tiny window with bars embedded

in the glass—it's a *state-of-the-art* facility.
I can see a bit of the eastern sky beyond.
The sky is dark purple and pink as the sun
comes up. They bring me breakfast in here
on a tray and I get to look at the wall while
I await transport to the courthouse, going
over and over what happened, wondering
what will happen next.

My father came to see me less than an
hour after I was arrested. It could be a
disaster for his career although he didn't
say that, which was unusually thoughtful
but good because it's not always about
him, right? They've always been just
the same that way, my mother and my
father, doing whatever they want and

expecting me to just go along with it, no say in anything, like I'm some sort of pet they've kept around the house, not worth consulting about anything, not ever asked how I want things.

Right away I noticed the stubble on his face. He hadn't even bothered shaving. Something had finally shaken his world up, like he was a little man that had come unglued from the bottom of a snow globe and now was floating around banging his head on the plastic walls, trying to get his feet glued back down again. He came in and he looked at me, his eyes all red. "Isabella. What happened? You have to tell me." I had my arms crossed and he leaned over and took my hand. It was the first time he'd touched me tenderly since I was ten years old, aside from patting me on the shoulder like I was the dog.

It's a long drive for him but he's been coming twice a week. I've seen him more than I ever did when we lived in the same house. He must like the routine here. He's all about routine. Every Sunday is visitor time although they've made some special arrangements for him to have an extra visit.

They do art therapy in here. And yoga. You have to go. *Mandatory* yoga. "What's Zen about that?" I asked the yoga instructor. Her name is Anna—it says that on her name tag that she wears, the red facility pass she has clipped to her yoga outfit, the pass that gives her access to the high security part of the facility. It's pronounced *Auna*, all drawn out like *awning* or *yawning*, which is what I want to do when I am forced to spend time with her. She keeps correcting us when we get it wrong. Another girl told her it was stupid to have a name pronounced a different way than it was spelled. *Auna* gave her a long cold look and then got a youth worker to come and take her away and she got locked up in her room, in her cell, for insolence. I'd like to come up behind her, grab her stupid ponytail and

give a yank and watch her neck snap. That
would be pretty funny yoga.

The art instructor is named Jane. Someone
called her Jane the Shit Stain to see what
she would do. She just smiled and said,
"Call me whatever you want, I don't care."
All the girls laughed. They don't have
anything else to do but laugh. They are
all sentenced. I'm the only one in here
on remand, on dead time, waiting for my
dumb court date. The stupid youth workers
told me they've seen other people sit for a
year in here waiting for their trial and then
they are found guilty and none of it counts
as time served, a whole year of dead time.
Jane comes every week. She's the only one

in here who is nice, who doesn't talk down to me. Art is the only thing I can stand. I want to be an interior designer. I picked out all the colors for our house after my mother left. My father wanted the whole place redone and he let me pick out the colors. Brighten the place up, he said. He hired a real interior design company but he told the head designer to work with me. He was away on a trip for most of it and I was there in that empty house in the country.

Yesterday in art therapy Jane got us to pick colors to reflect how we feel. She has this color wheel she uses, a poster she puts on the wall. Color therapy, she calls it. I pointed at all the shades of purple, and then to the deep plum purple. "Yes," she said, nodding. "What does it say about you, that color?" she asked.

What I think is this: I am all the colors of the sunrise and sunset, painted by a dark demon spirit who dwells in a stone tower on a cliff that looks out over a dark blue sea where only mermaids who have betrayed their kind now swim with sharks and strange creatures of the deep that never come to the surface. But I didn't say that. I just smiled and looked down. When I looked up, she was staring at me, her eyes these pale green pools, the pupils dark lilies.

"You can always talk to me, Isabella. About anything. I know you don't talk to the other girls and that you've had some trouble with the youth workers. It's hard having to be polite all the time. You must feel very alone." She smiled in this friendly way.

I could feel the panic crawling up my throat then, like some sort of horrible lizard. My eyes filled up with tears but I didn't say anything because I learned long ago that people don't really care and I wasn't about to trust her even though she seemed like she really felt bad for me—but it's all pretend, just like the rotten tooth fairy and that sort of shit. That's what growing up is about, learning that adults just lie their heads off, that growing up is about being just like them. This morning when I woke up I imagined a shelf running along the top of my cell with the head of every adult who has ever caused me a problem sitting on it like vases.

▬▬▬ ●

Sergei always told me he was a tough guy, I told the police. Talked about beating up losers. He was in court once for uttering death threats so I know they'll believe me.

Sergei's grandfather was Russian, born and raised in Moscow when it was a Communist country. Sergei told me that his grandfather was a spy and if he hadn't defected, Sergei could have been a Russian hockey star, because they have a better hockey program over there. At first I thought Sergei was telling the truth. He is so big, so strong. But then I found out his grandfather wasn't a Russian spy. He was a janitor at the American embassy in Moscow. Apparently the embassy let even janitors defect. But I suppose everybody has secrets, even janitors.

The truth is, Sergei smoked away his hockey career. They always told stories about him at school. That's what my father kept saying, too. Why can't you find someone who is your own age? You're only fifteen and he's nineteen. He can't even get out of high school. My father didn't understand that boys my own age are tedious. He told me he didn't want to see him around anymore.

I kept my end of the bargain. He never did see him—because I only had Sergei over when my father wasn't at home.

But then, if my father was really concerned about me, he would have stayed around a bit more, wouldn't he? I mean, teenagers will be teenagers, that's what everyone says. He always expects kids to act like adults. My grandmother died when I was little but I remember she said that when

he was a little boy he was always dressing
up in a suit, staying inside to count the
money in his piggy bank when the other
kids were outside climbing trees. When
he married my mother they went on their
honeymoon to a resort where he had a
conference so he could use the trip as a
tax write-off. She just sat on the beach the
whole time talking to the cabana boys.

▰▰ ●

My father's second visit here, I came in
to the visiting cell and he looked up at
me like he was going to chair a meeting.
He had a pad of paper and a pen. "Tell

me what happened. I'm getting you the best lawyer. I'll see that Sergei is put away forever." He was talking really fast. He was all business, just writing notes, doing damage control. Clean shaven. Not like the first time, when he still cared enough about me to be upset.

I said that Sergei was going to tell them what really happened. He wasn't all bad, I told him. I mean, who is all bad? Sergei wasn't going to let them put me away for something that he was responsible for. He promised when the police arrived at the pond that he would make sure they knew the truth, that I was innocent. Sergei would keep his word.

My father nodded, playing with his pen. It drove me crazy that he wouldn't even look me in the eye. It was like he didn't believe a word I was saying.

━━ •

It felt like Lulu was everywhere after that time we saw her at the store. We drove by her once and she was walking this big white poodle, and she gave us a big wave and smile, and of course she winked. I could see her, even though we were driving fast. He said there was no way I could have seen her from that far away, that I was starting to act crazy, really paranoid. Well, I felt my face turn red when he said that.

"Crazy? Me, crazy?" And I put my hand on the door handle and opened the door. "Maybe I'll just hop out right here. How about that? I'm sure my father would love to know you pushed me out of the car." Of course I would never have jumped out but Sergei didn't know that, did he?

He slammed on the brakes. "Isabella, are you out of your mind?"

"I know exactly what I'm doing. Don't you dare call me crazy. I'm not the one who's crazy for their ex-girlfriend, now am I?"

He said he wasn't but how was I supposed
to know if he was telling the truth, that's
what I said.

I miss Sergei's hands. Big, strong, warm.
They were always warm on my body,
moving so slowly. My Russian love
machine, I called him. I can see his hands
when I close my eyes, open like fans,
spread like sea stars on the sand.

He was always wanting me. But I only let
him when he was good, when he behaved,
when he did my chores around the house,
when he arrived exactly when I told him
to, and left when I told him to, when he
called or texted me when I told him to.
Then he'd get his reward.

I mean, he wasn't doing much with his life, just looking after his grandmother all the time but anyone can look after an old Russian lady. What's the big deal about that? I told him he was a loser, that he'd let his life just rot. He got so angry, so hurt. He wanted to get married but I told him I couldn't marry him like he was. And who gets married when they are fifteen? But Lulu, I bet she wanted to marry him. She would probably be into teen marriage, just to get her claws in him, to get Sergei away from me. She'd probably get pregnant right away and he'd be stuck with her for the rest of his life and that would be just fine with her.

My father didn't even know Sergei and
I were seeing each other, that's what he
told the police. He'd forbidden it. He
used to forbid a lot of things but it's hard
to rule the castle when you are never in
the kingdom, that's what I told him when
he came to see me here for the first time
three months ago, after they called him
and said I'd been arrested. I remember
my father sitting there, all tired looking,
rumpled. We were in a little room and
there was a youth worker sitting outside
the door.

"But I told you not to see him anymore,"
he said, looking at the bruise on my face,
putting his head in his hands.

"Yes, I know, Daddy. But I was lonely."
I looked at him and then down again. It
was easy to start crying. I used to practice
in my bedroom with a stopwatch to see
how quickly I could make my eyes fill up
with tears. I would think about starving
children in Africa, their bony bodies
and bloated stomachs, things like that. I
would sit there on my bed, holding my
pink princess mirror in one hand and the
stopwatch in the other and I would picture
poor little children, all alone, children in
those refugee camps with no parents, and
then the tears would slip over my eyelids
and run down my face. Just looking at
myself was amazing, how my eyes filled up

like fish bowls and the tears slid down in a perfect shape, how sad I looked. It was like watching a star in a movie, this really beautiful girl that no one understands and she's all alone all the time, her boyfriend's ex-girlfriend trying to steal him away.

After that I only had to picture my face and I could get the waterworks going right away. It took about sixty seconds at first but I got it down to thirty seconds after doing it every day for a week. I pushed up my sleeve again so my father could see the purple there, too, where Sergei had grabbed me, just as the tears started to fall. Perfect timing.

My father looked up, but not at me, at the beige wall. There were tears in his eyes and he couldn't stop them from coming out. The youth worker put a box of tissues on the table in between us.

▬▬▬ ●

I remember all those times in the front hall of our house, when my father would leave for evening meetings. He'd be on the way out the door and he'd say, "Now, Isabella, you do your homework. Stay off the phone. Don't be on the computer all night." I'd smile and he'd pat me on the cheek. *That's my girl.*

When he drove down the road I'd text
Sergei and he'd come over. My father
would always have these chores for me to
do every week, mow the lawn, weed the
garden. Sergei would do them while I sat
in a lawn chair. It was nice living in the
country, all that privacy. You could do
whatever you wanted. When Sergei's back
was turned I'd take my clothes off. He'd
turn around and his eyes would pop and
he'd run his tongue over his sexy red lips
and give me this hot little smile.

━━ ●

I was sad when my mother left, but I was

only twelve and three years is enough
time to get over it. She hated the house. It
had been my father's idea to move to the
country. He said the commute was worth
it for the peace and quiet. But she was
bored, sitting in a chair looking down over
the field to the valley below. She bought
a painting and hung it there by the big
window. It was all these pastel swirls with
words in them: *Soft winter white makes
pale winter blues.*

"Why are you going?" I'd asked her that
day when I got off the bus. My mother
was in the doorway with her suitcases.
It was early June. She'd forgotten it was
a half day at school and I came home to

find her packing up her car. "I'm so sorry," she said. That was all she had time for. I thought it was a joke until I found her note. For my father. I didn't get one.

"You'll be fine. You're just like him," she said, as she got into the car, smiling at me. Not a mean smile. A smile like it was the only thing she could do and, even though it was such a small thing, she felt good about it.

She was gone but that didn't mean my father was around more. It was like nothing had changed for him.

I was in the city once, on a school trip.

We got lost and we ended up at a hotel,
a fancy one in the city center. There was
a café in the middle of the lobby with all
these potted trees.

You could have a drink there or high tea
in the hotel café. There was a woman
sitting at a table and Susan, my classmate,
whispered that she was a hooker. She had
dyed blond hair and stiletto black boots. I
suppose she could have been a hooker. We
were sitting there and who came in and sat
down with her but my father. Susan didn't
know it was my father, though.

He didn't see me until we were leaving. I
was outside on the sidewalk and he saw

me through the glass wall. His eyes got huge. I just looked away and giggled with my friends as the bus pulled up for us. He got home late that night and I was already in bed. Of course I wasn't asleep but he didn't know that. He tried to bring it up the next day at breakfast but I just brushed him off and said I didn't care.

But I did care and I couldn't stop thinking about it. He had time to spend with her, some prostitute, but he never had time to spend with his own daughter. I mean, what is with women like that, not caring about anyone else, that my father might have responsibilities, that there might be someone more important than a cheap hooker. But people like her, they never care about anyone else. It's just about them and what they want. Just picturing her there with my father made me so mad. The nerve. Taking him away from me. I mean, she wouldn't be laughing if she was put in her place, would she? It would have served her right to have me come up to her and she'd look at me, like I was going to ask a question, and then I'd take out a hammer, just a little one like the kind they use for reupholstering furniture, and give her whore head a whack and see how long she was able to stand up on her high heels then.

The police wanted to know how I hooked up with Sergei. That was the term they used, *hooked up*. I tried not to laugh.

I'd seen Sergei around at school. He kept to himself. He wasn't much into school, really, just goofing off. He might've been a loser but he was the best-looking loser around. He was really tall and I heard he was in martial arts for a while too.

One day last June my dad dropped me off after an appointment with the orthodontist and Sergei was standing by the school door on the side having a cigarette. You aren't supposed to smoke on school property but Sergei never cared

about what you're supposed to do. I
walked by and he smiled and then, with
those big eyes of his, he winked. Well, I
winked right back at him, with my head
to the side all sexy, and just kept going.
I know he turned and watched me walk
away so I made it worth his while.

I was grocery shopping with my father the
day after and I saw Sergei in the parking
lot loading groceries in the trunk of a car
for this little old lady—his grandmother,
he told me later. And then I saw him
driving by when I was walking the dog.
I was just coming home and turning into
the driveway when he went by. He waved.
I stood there looking at him and then at

the last second I waved, and then I turned my head as he gave me this big smile.

The next day I walked by the north corner of the school where he hung out with the guys who always got in trouble and he was leaning there against the wall and gave me that lazy smile again. "Why are you stalking me?" I said. He just laughed. And all his friends started laughing. But his laugh wasn't mean—he just looked like he thought I was hilarious.

When he went by that night I was outside with my father, who was home early for once. I told my father he was following me, that he had this thing for me and wouldn't leave me alone. I was pretty sure he *did* have a thing for me, but I wanted to be completely sure. I wanted his complete attention.

My father waved him down. He started giving it to him, and then Sergei looked at him and said, "I live down the road, dude. You can't tell me what to do." And then he drove away really fast. My father was so pissed at me. It was so funny. But how was I supposed to know Sergei lived on our road? And so, later, when they questioned him, my father told the police that Sergei was obsessed with me. He didn't tell them how it really happened, that Sergei was just going to his house.

They didn't need that detail.

At school the next day Sergei came up to me. "Isabella," he said, "I think you're trouble."

"Oh, I'm trouble, am I?" I smiled and tossed my hair back. I had this new stuff in it that enhanced the curl.

He shook his head and smiled back. "Why did you tell your father I was stalking you?"

"Well, I thought you were. I never saw you on our road before."

Then he started laughing again. "It's not *your* road. We've been living on that road since way before you moved there. It's kind of sexy, your tunnel vision. The way you revolve around yourself like you are the sun and the moon," he said. And then he started laughing again. He has these big soft lips and chocolate cake eyes.

"Want me to come visit sometime when your daddy's away?" He leaned toward me and I could smell his warm skin.

"See, you *are* stalking me," I said, and I gave him the little smile I do in the mirror at home.

"Everyone wanted to know who was building that big-ass house. What was it, like five years ago? You were just a little girl then." He smiled with those soft red lips. "Are you all grown up now?"

"Wouldn't you like to know," I said in a soft little voice. I gave Sergei a wink and then walked away, saying "See you around sometime." The kind of voice my mother used to use on my father when I was in bed and they didn't think I could hear. They'd put the back deck too close to my room. I'd never do that. I'd put my kids' rooms in the basement so they couldn't hear anything.

After my mother left, I told my father I wanted to have the guest room as my room, at the front of the house on the

ground level. It was supposed to be a
sitting room but they didn't need it so
it became this extra guest room and no
one used it. He didn't care. That was
when we hired Bewitching Interiors, so
we had the room all done up in pink and
he got me a new canopy bed. I've got an
amazing bedroom. Cinderella Pink is the
paint color we used on the walls. Pink is
the color of pure love. The ceiling is Iced
Violet. It's supposed to be calming. Sergei
told me in Russia it's the color of the
dead. That pissed me off, him making my
nice room like a morgue. He was probably
making it up. It's not like he was born
there or anything. He doesn't even speak
Russian.

━━ •

When my mother left and my dad brought in Bewitching Interiors he let me make all the choices. He trusted me. *You have an eye for detail. You are all about the detail.* It's true. I am all about the detail, the trim, the edge, the look. The first thing I'd do in this stupid jail—sorry, *youth center*—is put some color on the walls. How can they expect people to make any changes in their lives with such dingy colors?

The interior designer came to our house. She brought all these paint swatches and took me to a special flooring store to pick out carpet. And we picked out fabric to have the furniture recovered. It was really gorgeous, just perfect. Every day when I'd come home from school one more part of the house would be finished. It looked like a new house. My father loved it. It was like we were papering right over my mother, painting her out of the picture, redesigning a world without her.

———

I finally let Sergei drive me home from school. My father was never home at that time of day so I wasn't worried. And sure enough, just when we got in the door my phone rang and it was my father: he had a meeting so he'd be home late, I should get something out of the freezer to make myself for supper.

Sleep tight, goodnight, goodnight, goodnight.

We went out on the deck looking out over the valley. He took out a joint. "You smoke?" I just shrugged and giggled. He lit up and then showed me how. He didn't even laugh when I coughed, just patted me on the back, and helped me take another toke. "You don't always get high the first time," he said. But next thing I knew my head was as light as flower petals and I was twirling around. I was wearing red shoes and he kept calling me Dorothy. It was spring and I could hear these evening birds and I took him by the hand into my canopy bed. He was so heavy and he said he didn't want to hurt me and then I couldn't stop laughing. "It's not the first time for everything, you asshole," I said, slapping him on the back. He was surprised and it was the funniest thing I ever saw. That's what I loved about being high, laughing my ass off.

"Come on, Russian," I said.

"Dorothy," he said, looking into my eyes. "Aren't you a bad girl."

"I'm not Dorothy," I told him. "I'm the

Wicked Witch of the West."

"You're fierce," he whispered with a huge
smile the next day when he saw me at
school. "My wicked witch."

I winked at him and he smiled.

And then we had this great thing all year,
him coming over and doing whatever
chores my father wanted done, and getting
high and having sex in my bedroom. Until
we were in the store and she came by,
that girl. I wish he'd never gone out with
her. She still wanted him. I could tell by
the way she looked at him. Lulu. What
a stupid name. Sergei says it's short for

Lucille. Nicknames are for freaks. No one
has ever called me anything but Isabella.
Once a teacher called me Izzy and I stared
at her until I thought I had frozen her to
ice. "Isabella," I said. "We don't shorten it.
Ever." The teacher bit her lip and nodded.
She never called me anything after that.

Lulu and Sergei never really went out,
he said. He just really liked her but it
was a couple of years ago. He had to do
community service work at the senior
citizens' home as a part of his sentence for
some crime he committed when he was
sixteen, and she volunteered there, taking

the old drooling people out for a bit of
fresh air. He had to work in the gardens
and so she'd go by pushing some old
vegetable in a wheelchair, I bet winking
her stupid eye at him while he killed all
those weeds.

But her name kept coming up after that
time we saw her in the store, for five
months it was like she was always there
with us. We went to a movie and when
we were buying popcorn the guy at the
popcorn counter asked Sergei if I was his
sister. And then he asked if Sergei had
seen Lulu lately, said that she was pretty
hot and he couldn't believe he let her get
away. That guy was lucky I didn't come

around the counter and stick his face in the boiling hot butter topping because nothing would have made me happier than seeing his skin blister and melt. I was so pissed I walked out of the theater and threw my popcorn all over the parking lot. Sergei tried telling me that the guy was just an idiot, that he was jealous because my father was rich.

And then once I went with him when he was buying groceries for his grandmother and there Lulu was at the end of the aisle, all little and cute, waving at him like she was sitting on a float in a dumb parade. I wanted to bash her head in with a can of peaches. And Sergei's grandmother, she just loved Lulu, asking about her whenever I was there, like she was disappointed every time I came in the door. She even called me Lulu once. I almost lost it but Sergei corrected her and told her I was Isabella. "Oh yes," she said, but I could tell from her voice she was disappointed, like she was hoping if she counted to three I'd transform into that stupid Lulu.

"I thought you said you never went out with her," I asked him. "So how does your grandmother know who she is?"

Sergei said he drove his grandmother to some social club for old people at the nursing home and Lulu would do crafts

with them sometimes, or read to them.
He said she played the flute and would do
little concerts for them.

Lulu, Lulu, tweeting away on her flute,
like some bird that won't shut up. She was
just doing whatever she could to get Sergei
back—and he was defending her.

I couldn't stop thinking about her, asking
him about her. I told him that I wasn't
going to have sex with him anymore,
that it was over unless he got rid of her.
I just wanted him to tell her to leave us
alone. To take a stand. I wanted her out
of our lives. Sergei kept saying she wasn't
a problem, I should just forget about her.

Well, how was I supposed to do that with
her popping up everywhere we went? How
was I supposed to believe him? I asked
him. How was he going to prove she
wasn't a problem?

I told Sergei if he didn't get her to stop
bugging me I'd tell my father he'd been
coming over every night for months, I'd
tell the police he was a drug dealer. And
no more touching my body. No more
Wicked Witch of the West ever again,
just Dorothy, and Dorothy isn't any fun.
He kept saying it was all in my mind,
that I was getting totally paranoid and
neurotic. Our town was so small we were
bound to run into her sometimes, he said.

She wasn't stalking him and he wasn't lying or hiding anything. But I could just tell. He said that was crazy. I'm not crazy. I just have this extra sense. I'm not like other people. I was so mad that he made it out like I had the problem.

It was the winking. If only she hadn't winked. Winking was *our* thing, I told Sergei when we got back to my house from the store. *Some things are supposed to be sacred*, I yelled at him. I couldn't get to sleep at night for months. I'd see her with her long hair and those big blue eyes, her sexy smile, those long lashes like feathers touching as she winked right in front of me. So I told him that he had to get rid of her.

"Well, I guess he took you literally," my father said when I first told him this. I nodded. Yes, that was what happened. Sergei took it literally.

I told my father and the police about the evening it happened. Sergei said we should go out, he wanted to take me out and show me something special. If I'd just come with him, he said, it would all be better.

I wanted to believe him. It was getting dark later now because it was June. It was a beautiful evening. The colors were gorgeous, all these different shades of purple and blue, just like eye shadow.

Sergei drove me to the woods near this pond where he said there were water lilies blooming, he was going to show me a surprise, prove his love to me. He was already high when he picked me up. He was on crack. That's not something I did. He's the drug addict.

We sat in his car and got really high and then walked in on this path through the trees. It was like being in a storybook. And then we came out into this beautiful clearing and the pond was reflecting the sunset as though the sun was in the water, like the water was magic. There was a snap and I looked up and who was there but her. She must have followed us. Lulu. The sun hit her hair and she was standing there with the deep green forest behind her like fucking Snow White. She took a few steps forward and smiled, all nervous, and said, "What was so important you needed to talk to me about, Sergei?" And then Sergei got crazy. "Are you following me?" he said. "I told you to leave me alone. I love Isabella, not you. Can't you accept that?"

"But Sergei, you told me to meet you here," she said. I told the police Lulu said that. And she started crying. "But I love you," she said to Sergei. I'm sure she said that. It sounded like that. It made me so mad.

It happened so fast. He went up to her and

grabbed her by that long hair and she fell down on her knees. And then Sergei kicked her in the side and Lulu bent over. She couldn't catch her breath. I was frozen at first. "See," he said to me, "I'm showing you." He kicked her in the eye, that winking eye. I was crying, saying he should stop. That's what I was doing. My hands are sweating, remembering this.

"Don't hurt her," I screamed. "I won't tell my dad you've been coming over. I won't tell him about the drugs. I was just kidding," I screamed.

But he was out of control. When she tried to get up he came behind her. She

was on her knees. He came behind her
and put out his hands, really slowly. She
wasn't moving fast so he wasn't rushing.
He held out his hands like he was going
to put them under her arms and help
her get up. But then he moved really
quickly and put them around her neck and
started to squeeze. She started wiggling,
thrashing around, making these horrible
sounds. I can hear them now, these little
gurgles, gasping for breath, and he just
squeezed even harder. She had on a fine
gold necklace and it wrapped all around
his finger so tight it cut right into him but
he just kept going. Violence takes the pain
away. The necklace wasn't on her neck

when they pulled her out of the pond. It
must have fallen off in the water. It's a
deep pond. The police never mentioned it.
I grabbed his arm to get him to stop, and
that's when he spun around and hit me in
the face and I fell down.

I started crying when I told my father
this when he first came in with all his
stubble. I cried when I told the police and
my lawyer, every time I've told them. My
nose was running, snot all over my face, all
over my bruised cheek. It was disgusting.
Crying is disgusting. The youth worker
who came in to see if everything was okay
was this really cute guy and I didn't want
him to see me like that. After he left, my

father reached across the table and put his hand on my shoulder. "It's okay, Isabella," he said. "We'll get through this. This is my fault for not being around more... I'm so sorry." His voice broke and I took my hands down from my face so he could see me, my eyes red and blotchy. There were tears running down his cheeks as he held my hand.

━━ ●

After my mother left I used to wonder what she would have looked like if the brakes hadn't worked on her car, after she left me standing there and drove out of our lives, what her face would have looked like if

it had smashed through the windshield,
glass stuck in her big sparkling eyes.

For the last year when my mother called
for our Sunday talk I didn't bother
answering the phone. She finally called my
father at work. He told me I should really
find time to take her call. I just shrugged
and said I'd see what I could do. He
sighed. "Isabella, when your mind is made
up it's like trying to stir dried concrete." I
thought that was stupid because concrete
is so ugly and I felt like kicking him.

But here I am, surrounded by concrete.
I told the warden how ugly this place
is and it was the one time he laughed.

"Why would we want to pretend you are somewhere pleasant?" he asked me. "This isn't a boarding school, Isabella. This isn't a hotel. Or some storybook palace. You need to grow up and take responsibility for yourself." I would have liked to have shoved chopsticks in his temples, nice and slow, right into his brain.

"Whatever," I said.

Sergei and I were standing by the pond and Lulu was lying there, dead. I was hyperventilating. Then Sergei came over to me and started to kiss me, I told the police. He was crazy, all pumped up on drugs and from the adrenaline. It surges through your body. I was still really stoned and I felt dizzy. When we first got there and parked, he took out this joint and we smoked it. It made my lungs burn. I don't know what he had in it but there was a funny taste in my mouth, and I could feel my heart go faster, like every hair on my body was standing up a bit, like my skin could feel every single bit of the wind, the warmth of the sun, like it was all magnified and it was like I was ten feet tall except my head felt like a balloon that was going to float up and away any second. And then it was like I was floating outside of myself, darting all around, a dragonfly, watching myself as we walked to the pond.

And then it all happened and we were there with her at our feet. My heart was pounding and I was dripping sweat. I pushed him away and we stood there looking at each other. A frog croaked from the water and we both looked at the pond. And then she started moaning. She wasn't dead. I couldn't believe it, all those kicks, being strangled like that, and still alive. I told Sergei he had to stop, that he couldn't cross that final line. "Just a kick to her head," he said. "That's all it will take." She sort of crawled, but she went the wrong way, toward the pond. She got up and was wobbling. And then Sergei walked over and gave her a push with his foot and she fell in. That's all it took, a little tap. I would have jumped in to save her but the pond looked really deep. She didn't struggle much, just floated there, face down among the water lilies with the sun setting on her long hair.

And that's when those nature people came hiking out of the woods on some evening songbird outing. They had a cell phone and called the police. I was at the edge of the pond holding a big stick when they saw me. I was only trying to drag her to land. They backed up like they thought I was going to hit them with it. Sergei ran

away into the trees and I followed him.
It was dark with all the leaves overhead.
He lit a cigarette. I told him he'd have to
take responsibility. It was then that he said
he would tell the truth, he would make
sure they knew it was him. I ran back out
crying, asking the nature people to help
me while the Lulu bird floated in the
water and Sergei ran away to his car.

━━━ ●

I can hear them coming down the hall now.

The door opens and the sheriff is standing
there with cuffs and shackles. "Time to
go for a ride," he says, nodding at me,

no smile. "Stand up please and put your hands behind your back."

I stand up and face that ugly beige wall.

I was looking at this same wall the first time I talked to my lawyer. He was telling me that the police were interviewing Sergei for the millionth time, that if the judge accepted Sergei's testimony they'd drop the charges when I came to court to enter a plea.

The metal snaps together as they put the cuffs on. They don't say anything about my sweating hands. The shackles take longer. I'm just standing there, being cooperative.

The shackles catch on the leg of my gray sweatpants. The sheriff apologizes to me. "It's okay," I say, looking at the wall.

And just then, the warden comes in. He clears his throat, that's how I know it's him. "Your lawyer just called. Your friend Sergei is going to testify," he says.

I smirk. *Tell me something I don't know*, I think.

But then he does. "He says that you killed that girl, that he couldn't go through with it so you did it and he hit you, he tried to stop you," he says in his flat voice. "It's true, isn't it?"

I don't say a word.

Instead, I smile.

Smile at the beige wall.

"They dredged the pond and found the necklace." The warden clears his throat again. "They are charging you with murder in the first degree."

I keep right on smiling because I'm going to stick a knife in Sergei's gut as soon as I get my hands on him and I can't wait to see his face then. I should have known he wouldn't keep his word. You can't trust Russians.

I'll see him at the courthouse. I'll make him feel pain like he has never felt pain

before and he'll be afraid to even think my
name for the rest of his pathetic life.

I think about my father's face that very
first time I saw him in this place, the
morning after Lulu died. He was so tired.
He closed his eyes and then opened them
—and then he opened them wider as
he looked at my hand on the table. He
reached out and ran his pen along the
inside of my index finger where there
was a deep cut like a red thread running
from the bottom of my finger to the top.
"Where did you get that cut, Isabella?" he
asked, his voice almost a whisper. I looked
at him then just like I'm looking at the
warden now—with eyes full of beige.

Single Voice

Jen Sookfong Lee

Shelter

I didn't know.
The words repeat in Abby's mind.
Idiot. How could you be so stupid?
Abby's mother goes clubbing and
her father works obsessively, while
responsible Abby makes dinner and
watches out for her sisters.
Then she meets Sean, who works at
the animal shelter where she volunteers.
Animals trust you, he says.
Abby wants to melt into him. Sure,
he's older, but he understands her
when it seems no one else does.
Abby falls hard for Sean. She wants
to make him love her back, but her
fantasy romance takes a very wrong turn.

annick press
toronto + new york + vancouver

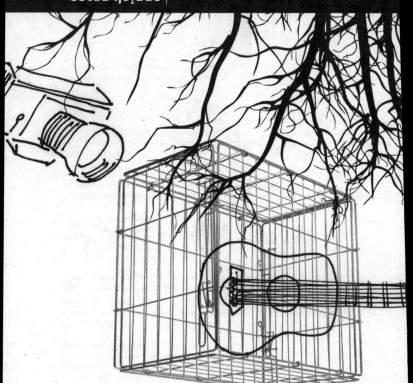

Shelter

Jen Sookfong Lee

Single Voice

© 2011 Jen Sookfong Lee

Annick Press Ltd.

All rights reserved. No part of this work covered by the copyrights hereon may be repro-
duced or used in any form or by any means—graphic, electronic, or mechanical—without
prior written permission of the publisher.

Series editor: Melanie Little

Copyedited by Geri Rowlatt
Cover design by David Drummond/Salamander Hill Design
Cover photo (cage) by WilleeCole / shutterstock.com
Interior design by Monica Charny

We acknowledge the support of the Canada Council for the Arts, the Ontario Arts
Council, and the Government of Canada through the Canada Book Fund (CBF) for our
publishing activities.

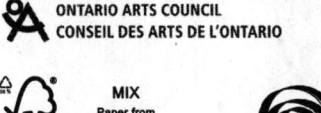

ONTARIO ARTS COUNCIL
CONSEIL DES ARTS DE L'ONTARIO

MIX
Paper from
responsible sources
FSC® C004071
www.fsc.org

ANCIENT FOREST ™
FRIENDLY

Annick Press is committed to protecting our natural environment. As part of our efforts, the
text of this book is printed on 100% post-consumer recycled fibers.

Published in the U.S.A. by
Annick Press (U.S.) Ltd.

Distributed in Canada by
Firefly Books Ltd.
66 Leek Crescent
Richmond Hill, ON
L4B 1H1

Distributed in the U.S.A. by
Firefly Books (U.S.) Inc.
P.O. Box 1338
Ellicott Station
Buffalo, NY 14205

Visit our website at www.annickpress.com
Visit Jen Sookfong Lee at www.sookfong.com

I didn't know. Every time I close my eyes
against the trees and grass of this sad little
park, that same thought runs through
my head like a mean-spirited whisper. *I
didn't know.* I want to cry, but there's a
man feeding pigeons twenty feet away
and if he asks me what's wrong, I might
crumple into a ball at his feet. And then
what would he do? Try to call my parents?
Run away? Or maybe he might hold me,
his meaty, crumb-covered hand on my

shoulder. My stomach churns and I think I might start sobbing anyway, but I swallow hard and stare at the sky, streaky and red from the sunset.

The dark is coming. It's getting colder every minute, but the cold is good. In the cold, people cover up their ears and look at their shoes while they hurry through small parks like this, the ones with trash cans full to the brim with disposable coffee cups and Styrofoam lunch containers. They don't notice much, which means I'm just another lump that could be a shrub, a person, even a newspaper box. If I could become one with this bench, I would.

I sit on my hands to keep them from shaking. But this surging in my chest won't stop and I think of my mother's soft belly, the wrinkles in her skin where her stomach expanded and deflated three times, once for me and twice more for my sisters. I want to rest my head right there and breathe in her perfume that always reminds me of firelight and roses and cinnamon. My mother, who will probably not be home by the time I get there.

I'm crying now—harder than I've ever cried in my life. My body feels like it's melting from the inside out, like my organs have liquefied and are seeping through my eyes and ears. If I sit here

in the cold much longer, maybe I'll just freeze over and none of this will matter.

The man feeding pigeons is staring at me, but there's nothing I can do except hope that this storm of snot and coughing will soon be over. *Idiot*, I think to myself. *How could you be so stupid?* I don't understand. I'm Abigail Young, the girl who plans everything, who is never caught by surprise. I am never the girl who doesn't know. How did I become such a mess?

Explain it to me, I tell myself, *like it's a story*. Maybe then it will all make sense.

One week ago

I am in love with Sean.

His face was in my head when I woke up
this morning. Even now, while I'm making
peanut butter and banana sandwiches for
my sisters and trying to remember if today
is the day that Dad comes home at eleven
or just goes straight from the hospital to
his second job at the mall, Sean's voice
whispers in my ear. *Animals just trust you*,
he says. *See how they let you touch their
paws?* I want to curl up in his voice, pull
it over me like a blanket, and let his words
burrow their way into my skin.

Sometimes, when I think about love, I imagine the kind you see in movies where two people look at each other and their eyes seem to dissolve into their faces and you can feel the tension, those little sparks zipping between them. When I was younger and watched movies like that with my sisters, I would wonder if love really could travel across a room from your body to a stranger's until the two of you were hopelessly entangled. Or if someone you knew suddenly looked different to you one day, like the way ice cream tastes gross early in the morning but by the afternoon it's all you want.

Sean is my ice cream.

I hear the bathroom door slam and
one of my sisters swearing at the other.
Some days, I just want to lie down in my
bedroom and never come out. I could
stare at the ceiling and shut my ears to the
rest of the house. The front door opening
and closing behind my parents. Elizabeth
yelling at Chelsea to stop stealing her nail
polish. The crash of music from the laptop,
shoes hitting the floor, water glasses
overturning when the cat jumps up on the
dining-room table.

Five years ago, it wasn't like this. Back
then, my mother picked us up from school
and asked us how our day went while
we ate her signature snack: toast with

butter and honey and cinnamon, cut into perfect little triangles. When Dad came home, she started dinner and he helped us with our homework and told us funny stories, like how he was trying to fix a radiator at the hospital but a patient kept rummaging through his toolbox looking for scissors so he could cut his roommate's toenails, which were so long and yellow the thought of them kept him up at night. Later, after Chelsea had gone to bed, my parents turned on the radio and danced to whatever sappy pop song was playing, and Dad would say to Liz and me, "Isn't she beautiful, girls? I swear, she looks younger and younger every day." Mom would laugh

and pretend she was embarrassed, even
though I knew she loved it.

Now, my father works all the time and
my mother usually styles hair at the salon
until at least eight o'clock, when she's not
out with the younger women who work
there. I'm the one who makes spaghetti for
dinner and wakes up early every morning
to be sure my sisters leave for school on
time. And nobody dances around the
living room anymore.

Before Mom started working so late
and hanging out with her new friends,
I'd sometimes catch her staring at the
three of us and at Dad's empty chair and

then shrinking into the couch, as if her breath was leaving her, bit by bit. One day I watched her flipping through a pile of bills on the kitchen counter, her lips moving silently as she went from phone to electricity to credit cards. When I asked her if she wanted some help with the calculator or something, she glared at me and said, "Do you have any idea how much money it takes to keep this family going?" She waved her checkbook in the air like she was swinging an axe. "All this saving and working is so you and your sisters can go to a good school. It's what your father wanted—I hope you appreciate it." I've never heard her talk about money since then, but sometimes I can hear

that pitch in her voice, like she blames us but doesn't want to say the words. That is, when she's home.

Last week, while she was putting on her going-out makeup in the bathroom and chattering about the clubs and the other girls and how they gave each other pedicures in Michelle's apartment the other night, I could feel my head swelling, as if all the heat from the rest of my body was bubbling up. I couldn't stand my mother's voice—that high, excited tone that made her sound younger than Chelsea, who's the youngest. Finally, I just blurted out, "How much does all this cost, Mom? The drinks? The cover? The cabs?"

She turned around and looked at me with narrowed eyes. At first, I thought she was going to say something mean, but she sighed instead. "It's called ladies' night, Abby. Besides, I meet a lot of people at these clubs, including men who like to buy cocktails."

"Men?"

"Yes, men."

"But you're married!"

"Calm down, Abby. Nothing happens. It's just harmless fun."

"Do the men know how old you are?" I could tell I'd hurt her because she breathed

in and out twice before answering me, like she did when I was little and had taken a bite out of Liz's birthday cake before the party even started.

"Why are you being such a brat all of a sudden?"

Who was the brat here? Me or *her*? I was so angry I could hardly see; my mother was just a bright blur—glittery and shiny. I wanted to shake her, make her see this couldn't be right, that married women with teenaged daughters didn't accept Paralyzers from men they hardly knew. Instead, I spat out, "What would Dad say if he knew all that?"

She turned her back to me and shrugged before saying, "Yesterday he told me I looked like a slut." Her eyes met mine in the mirror. "And then he left for work, like he always does. Is that what you wanted to hear?"

Her lips trembled as she struggled to untwist the lid on her mascara, and I should have felt sorry for her—but I didn't. I put my hand on the doorknob and said, not quite under my breath, "Well, he's right. I bet those men in the bar think you're an old cougar."

She slammed her fist on the counter. "You're not going to be young forever either, you know. Look at you—you

already act like you're fifty and you've given up trying to have fun." She took a breath as if she wanted to say more, but I shot past her into the hallway. There was no way I was going to listen to her sneer at me when I'm trying harder than anyone else to keep this house running.

I could hear her calling after me. "Abby, Abby. Don't run away like that." She sounded sorry and weak, which made me even angrier. At least when I shut the door, I couldn't hear her anymore.

So really, I know she's lonely and angry and just wants to feel young again so she can forget this house and those bills. I

try to fix the snacks and cook dinner at
the right time like she used to and if I
had any funny stories, I'd tell them. But
somehow, even doing my best feels wrong
and hollow, and my sisters are still bitchy
and rude. Maybe I'm the only one who
remembers what it used to be like. Maybe
I'm the only one who cares.

▬▬ ●

It's Sean who actually listens to me like
I have something to say. I've only known
him for a month, but it feels like he's
always been a part of me, like an elbow or
the mole on my right shoulder.

Chelsea actually talked to him first—
which is typical, because she's the one with
the pretty face, the kind where everything
is smooth and even and sweet. My mother
once said that Chel will break hearts when
she's older. Then she looked at me and
said, "But you're the reliable one, honey,
and that's just as good."

If Sean thinks that's all I am, he's never
said so. But I know he sees more in me—
maybe that's why I love him.

That day, Chelsea was waiting for me by
the front reception desk at the animal
shelter—she usually stopped by on her
way home from basketball practice. I'd

been volunteering at the shelter for a few months and already knew my way around. The dogs even recognized my smell, and they barked when they heard me open and close the gate to the kennels.

When I walked out to the reception area, my sister was there, watching an older guy I'd never seen before spinning her basketball on his finger. She was laughing, her hazel eyes crinkled up, her smile perfectly cute. I sighed to myself. Whenever I smile, I show too much gum.

When Chelsea saw me, she stood up. "Hey, Abby."

I expected the guy to ignore me or maybe just nod in my direction, but instead he tucked the basketball under his arm and held out his other hand. "Hi—I'm Sean, the new night supervisor." He held my hand lightly, like he was afraid he might break it.

"Hi," I said quietly. I looked at my shoes for a second, wondering what I should say or if I should say anything at all. Finally, I pointed to the basketball. "Do you play?"

"I used to when I was in high school, but I wasn't very good. I just joined the team to impress the girls." He laughed. "Didn't work, though. I almost never got off the

bench." I could feel myself blushing, while Chelsea giggled like she'd been flirting with grown men her entire life.

For the first week or so after that, I didn't see a lot of Sean—my shift usually ended before his began. But then, he started coming in a little earlier. He always smiled when he saw me. It was a shining smile, a real smile.

One day I was getting the dogs their kibble—two cups each for the big dogs, one cup for the little yappy ones who always nipped at my feet when I set the bowls down—and wondering how much longer I could volunteer here. Even if

I only worked at a fast-food restaurant once a week, it might cover one of the house bills. But then I stared at the row of carefully measured bowls and thought, *But I love it here. I never want to leave.*

That was the day Sean and I began to talk for real. He sat down and asked me why I volunteer at the shelter, with this open smile on his face—as if he didn't expect anything in particular and just wanted to know what I would say. I told him that I liked the order of the place. Each animal with its own kennel. Feeding schedules posted on the bulletin board. The only time things change are when an animal is adopted or a new one is brought in.

"How about you?" I asked him, suddenly embarrassed that I'd revealed so much.

"I actually did a business degree, but I've always liked animals, so when this came up, I went for it. It feels a lot better to help a bunch of cats and dogs than to help a bunch of rich people get richer. And who can resist the puppies?" He grinned and my stomach flipped.

After that, whenever I'd see him, he'd ask me how I was feeling and I would tell him. One day, I even told him how my parents were never home and how whenever Chelsea tried to help me with dinner, Liz would distract her by picking a fight. And

he'd say he understood. I knew it wasn't crap. He really did.

Walking home after my shift, I could still see the way his lips moved and always seemed to be on the verge of smiling, as if he knew something was funny but didn't want to tell anyone just yet. His blond hair spun and curled around his head, looking like caramel in some lights and gold in others. I wondered if he smelled like candy. It was impossible to ignore. I was falling in love.

Three days ago

As we pull on our sneakers in the front

hall, Liz gives me a little push. "You're standing in front of the closet," she says. "Do you mind getting out of my way?"

Sometimes my sisters act like little kids, as if what they need is the only important thing in the world. I half expect Liz to stick out her foot so I can tie her shoe. I lock the door behind us and we walk to school, through the same streets with the same trees and the same row of family cars parked on either side. I glance back at our house, which is nice enough but looking shabbier every year. My mother's right. We may live in a safe neighborhood and go to a good school, but we can barely afford it. Nobody knows that we don't own

the house and just rent, or that my father has two jobs, or that my mother buys our clothes from film sets for seventy-five percent cheaper than she could get them anywhere else. All they know is that we're the Young family—glamorous-looking mother, strong-jawed father, three fresh-faced teenaged daughters.

I've been at this school for four years but I still feel the same way I did on the first day my mother dropped us off—like an alien. Most of the kids have lived in this neighborhood their whole lives, and go home to nannies and clean houses with scented candles on the counters. They'll never know what it's like to watch your

family coming apart while you try to keep
things together without losing your mind.

I take a deep breath while Chelsea pulls
open the door to the school. My sisters
walk in ahead of me, saying nothing. Soon
enough, the crowd in the hallway swallows
them up and I'm standing alone.

After class, I see Liz in a corner of the
soccer field. She's smoking. Three other kids
huddle around her, their hoods drawn up.
I walk over and poke her in the shoulder.

"You look like a poseur," I whisper in her ear.

She looks at me, eyes half closed, and
shakes her head. With all that black

eyeliner, she could be thirty instead of fifteen. "You look like a prude." She turns away and takes another drag off her cigarette. Her friends, none of whom I've ever heard speak more than a single word at a time, snicker.

I start to walk away, but then turn around. "I'm going to the shelter for a couple of hours," I call over to her. "If you want to eat, be home by six." As I make my way through the damp field, I hear her group restart their conversation—or what passes for conversation with them.

"My sister is a control freak."

"What?"

"Nothing."

"Whatever."

They're geniuses. I expect them to start cloning each other any minute.

At the shelter, Sean is sitting on the floor in one of the kennels, a water bowl wedged under his knee. Atlas, the German Shepherd-Newfoundland cross, lies on his side with his head in Sean's lap, his long pink tongue hanging out of his mouth. I wonder how Sean can sit with him like that; Atlas is a hundred pounds at least and the only dog here that scares me. He took a

chunk out of a Schnauzer's stumpy tail once before anyone could pull him off. But right now, his ears twitch and Sean strokes them until the dog's eyes start to close.

I am half-hidden by a concrete pillar. I know it's weird to stand here, staring at a man and a dog like some sort of stalker, but I can't move. I can see the blond hairs on Sean's arms and the dimple in his cheek as he smiles at that lucky mutt. My chest feels like it's been coated with hot fudge from the inside out, and I want to be warm and slow and dopey like this forever. I even imagine curling up beside them, right there on that cold floor, and shuddering when Sean reaches down and touches me. I stare

at the gold in Sean's hair and at his long fingers, and I don't want to just lie beside the dog—I want to *be* that dog. I wonder if I need professional help.

Of course, Sean chooses that moment to look up, and my face burns, fast and uneven. But I can't run away now, so I pretend that standing here is the most normal thing in the world, that my red, spotty face is part of a completely regular day, and that watching the dog is exactly what I should be doing.

I step forward and, in as flat a voice as possible, say, "Is Atlas ready for his walk?"

Sean shakes his head and looks down at the giant furry head in his lap. "He's been antsy for the last few days, so I thought some one-on-one time would help. I don't want to disturb him now that he's finally relaxed. I can walk him later myself."

Now that he's seen me, I can't stay and just gape at him. Instead I mutter, "Sure, whatever you want." I've totally forgotten what I've been told to do, so I stumble down the aisle between the kennels and push open the door to the staff washroom. I turn on the flickering fluorescent light and sit on the toilet, my hands folded in my lap. This is ridiculous. I've suddenly become a quasi-speechless, idiotic obsessive who

crouches in shadows and stares at a man
who barely knows I exist. I pull on the
ends of my hair and tell myself to chill out.
There's really only one thing to do.

I have to make Sean love me back.

I know he wants a girl who could save
the world, the kind of girl who passes out
hamburgers to homeless people and hums
while she sorts through the recycling. He
wants a girl who isn't afraid of a dog, even
an anxious, one-hundred-pound dog that
was abused as a puppy. I get up and leave
the washroom, knowing what I have to do.

I have to be the girl he wants.

I stand at the door to Atlas' kennel. Sean is walking down the narrow aisle toward me, his head bent over a clipboard. Quickly, I step in and crouch down to pat the thick ruff of fur around the dog's neck. Atlas stares at me, his large, red-rimmed eyes blinking slowly. For a moment, I'm scared he'll bite off one of my fingers, but instead he noses my arm upward so I can rub the top of his head. I speak softly in his ear, "Help me out here, buddy." He cocks his ears and sniffs my cheek. Then, without warning, he barks so loudly and deeply that I fall backward into his bowl of water. I swear Atlas is laughing as he paws at my foot, dripping drool onto my jeans.

Sean steps in and looks at the dog, at me, at the water running into the floor drain. "Is something the matter?" he asks. Concern lines his beautiful, heartbreaking face, but the corners of his mouth twitch when he sees me lying in a puddle of spit-scented water. He doesn't laugh, but I can tell he wants to.

I scramble up and brush my hands over my thighs. "No, no—we were just hanging out." I want a giant hand to reach into the kennel and carry me far, far away. Maybe Samoa. Or the South Pole.

"Alright—but in case you're looking for the new sponge mop, it's in the front office." And he turns around and begins

walking back the way he came, flipping
through papers and tapping a pen against
his smiling lips.

"Wait," I call out. I run after him and tap
him on the shoulder. "Do you like tuna?"

He raises one eyebrow. "Tuna?"

I've gone too far to stop now. I breathe
deeply and say, "I found this weird recipe
in one of my grandmother's old cookbooks
for tuna casserole made with potato
chips on top. I mean, who eats like that
anymore, right? So I thought I'd make it
tonight for dinner with my sisters just to
see if it's gross or if it's so gross it's actually

really, really good. If you like tuna, you
could stop by. That is, if you like tuna."

I'm not sure what possessed me, or why I
didn't shatter into a million pieces from
the stress of getting all that out. *I've never
done this before*, I think. *Please answer me.*

Sean looks at the skylight above us. When
his eyes meet mine again, I feel myself
leaning in toward him, as if my body
is being pulled in by his, like dust to a
vacuum. Quickly, I brace myself on the
wall with my left hand. He smiles.

"I'm a vegetarian."

Of course. I should have known. So much

for being the girl who could save the world.

"Yeah, tuna's really not for everyone anyway," I mutter. "Like olives." I turn around and hurry toward the staff room. It doesn't take me long to grab my bag and jacket and run out the back door.

The sun is setting earlier and earlier now and as I cut through the parking lot of a strip mall, hundreds of crows are flying east in a black cloud, cawing as they dip and flap through the darkening sky. Every night they gather on the roof of some home renovation store, coating the squat building with a breathing, vibrating black carpet. I guess they sleep together, wing

to wing, because they feel safe that way—
because owls or cats or speeding trucks
can't get to them. Maybe they're right. At
least they're never lonely.

Now Sean thinks I'm an idiotic tuna-
exploiter, a kid with a ridiculous crush
that we'll both soon forget. But he doesn't
know that I feel him in my gut, as if a
miniature Sean is parked in my abdominal
cavity, keeping me warm when I'm alone.
He doesn't know, and for some reason that
hurts almost as much as not having him. I
can't stand that he might think this means
only a little to me when it really means
everything. I look up. The cawing drowns
out my thoughts as I step through my

front gate. I should make dinner.

Chelsea pokes at the casserole with her
fork. Liz has stopped pretending to eat
and sits at the table with an open vampire
novel in front of her. The crumbled potato
chips on the top of the casserole are soggy
and gluey, like the paste we made when
I was in grade two from flour and water.
And the tuna smells like dirty gym socks.

"You won't hurt my feelings if you throw it
out," I say as I stand up. "There's probably
something you can heat up in the freezer."
I sigh as I scrape almost the entire casse-

role into the garbage. I hate wasting food.

Liz looks up and blinks at me. "Thank God. That was awful. Right up there with that time you tried to make *boeuf bourguignon*. Remember how Chel was all drunk from the cooking wine and then threw up?"

"And that was for Dad's birthday, too." Chelsea throws her plate into the sink and bits of tuna fly onto the backsplash. Before I say anything, she hastily wipes off the mess with a paper towel. "I'll do the dishes, Abby. Don't worry."

As I leave the kitchen, I hear Liz say, "You're such a suck-up, Chel. If Abby wants to do all the work, let her."

"I'm just trying to help, Liz."

"Why? It's not like she has anything better to do with her lame-ass life."

"And what's better? Standing around smoking weed all day?"

"Shut the hell up. What do you know?"

I watch as Liz stomps down the hall to the front door. She pulls up the hood on her sweatshirt just as I hiss at her, "Go ahead. Leave like you always do."

She turns to look at me, her black-lined eyes like cigarette burns. Her fists are balled up and, for a moment, I think she

might hit me, but instead she punches
open the unlocked front door and hurtles
down the steps into the night. Liz's words
linger in my head, pinging and squealing
and poking all the soft and tender bits,
those spots that hurt the most when
someone touches them. She goes out to
forget. I stay home to remember. In the
end it's the same thing.

Maybe I'll leave, too, just open the front door
and never come back, taking my lame-ass life
with me. If I'm so pathetic, they can manage
without me. I think how nice it would be just
to walk and walk and walk, first on sidewalks
stained with coffee and grease and gum, and
then on footpaths that wind through little

pockets of forest. Eventually, I'd get to the mountains, where the animals and I could breathe the same air, friendly and wordless. I lie down on my bed with my hands behind my head. But the speckled ceiling looks nothing like an open night sky. Just bumpy drywall that never changes.

An hour later, I wake up when I hear the garage door. My parents are rushing through the house, dropping shoes and bags and jackets as they go. Chelsea's voice cuts through the wall.

"But Dad, you promised you'd come to the game tomorrow."

My father mutters something I can't quite make out but it sounds negative. Chelsea still stupidly believes our parents will do what they say, even though they never do. Someone knocks on my door.

"Abby? It's Mom."

When she opens the door, I see she's wearing her clubbing outfit—tight black jeans, off-the-shoulder top, red stilettos. Her eyes flicker over my desk and bookshelves, anywhere but my face. We haven't talked much since our big fight. Not that I've wanted to.

"I bought groceries for the next few days and put them in the fridge. There are some

fig cookies if you need a treat." She forces a stiff smile and tries to keep her voice light. "I'm off to meet the girls now. How do I look?"

I let my head fall back on my pillow. "I don't know. Ridiculous?"

She raises an eyebrow. "What?"

"You look ridiculous, Mom. The only thing you're missing is a bad facelift." The words are like hot steam, pushing and pushing against my lips until I have to release them into the air. I keep asking myself the same questions: *Why doesn't she stay home with us? Why aren't we good enough?*

"Don't talk to me like that, Abby. I'm your *mother*."

"Then you should act like one." Her face falls underneath all that bright makeup, and I turn over so I can't see her anymore. I hear her swallow before she answers me.

"Don't think you're the only one who's unhappy around here. Do you know how it feels to spend all day making other women look beautiful when they barely say a dozen words to me? And then to come home to hear my husband criticizing the way I look, when he bothers to speak at all? I'm not dead yet, you know. I deserve some fun."

As she turns to leave, I mutter, "So do I." She pauses for a second as though she's about to say more, but then walks out, her perfume wafting behind her like a woodsy ghost.

Sean creeps into my mind again and I start to feel better. I can see his face when he looked at Atlas, a look of care and peace and contentment, a look that meant he was happy with the place he was in and had no fears about the world falling apart. I've seen that look before. A long time ago, I remember lying on the couch with my head in my mother's lap, my father reading to us from the newspaper. Liz sat on the floor by our feet and Chelsea dozed off in the beanbag chair, her small hand on my

father's knee. Back then, it always seemed to be cold and we had wood burning in the fireplace—the only thing that worked in the old house we used to live in. That house stood crookedly on a street that was never clean or orderly, but it didn't matter because at night everything in our living room was quiet and perfect and nice.

Sean understands how much all that matters. No one could look that way at an unwanted dog and not understand.

Just then, I hear my father's voice in the hall. "Abby? I'm leaving for work in ten minutes. Did you make any sandwiches today?" I get up and open the door and

Dad is tightening his belt, the lines on his forehead creased as he squints in the dim light. "Don't worry if you've got too much to do, sweetheart. I think your mother bought some frozen meat pies I can take with me." But he knows and I know that Liz and my mom are the only ones who like those pies, so I walk to the kitchen, even though all I want to do is tell him he should be worrying about making Mom and the rest of us happy again, even if we have to live somewhere else. Instead, he just stands there, smoothing the sleeves of his work shirt, his thin body tensed and tired, and I turn away because the sight of him makes me want to cry.

I'll go back to the shelter and try again.
Sean will love me. He has to.

Earlier today

I'm cleaning a cut paw on one of the cats.
Sean hasn't arrived yet, but he's been coming
in around four lately, so I wait, one eye on
the door to the front office. The orange cat
meows when I touch its wound with the
tip of the cotton swab. "Shhh. It'll be over
soon. I promise." She tries to pull her paw
away, but I hold on tight and she gives up
and lays her head on the floor of her cage.
When I'm done, I rub the spot between
her eyes and she purrs, ears twitching.

"She likes you." Sean's voice is right behind

me. Before I turn around, I take a deep breath and think to myself, *Don't mess it up. Be the girl he wants.*

"She's not that picky," I say as I smile. "I gave her a liver treat and now I'm her long-lost best friend."

He laughs. "And people say animals are loyal. Really, they're just hungry." As he turns to walk to the staff room, he says, "But at least there's no bullshit. What you see is pretty much what you get."

You are so right, I think, though I don't know how to say it without sounding too intense. But he seems to sense my

agreement. "Not like people, that's for sure," he says. "There aren't many people I want to see all the time."

"That's why I like it here," I say as I close the door to the kennel.

Sean stops walking and nods. "I know. Me, too." He pauses. "You're alright, though. I've been here a month and you haven't started annoying me—yet."

"Right back at you," I say. Something's exploded inside me and I can't see the room anymore, just sparks of color and a swirl of light that dances in from the window. I think I might topple over.

Later, I'm in the back room folding towels still warm from the dryer when Leah, a girl who volunteers one day a week, walks in holding a blanket balled up in her hands. "One of the dogs had an accident," she says, wrinkling her nose. She tosses the blanket into the washer and hurries over to the sink to wash her hands.

When she's done, she looks at me. "Hey Abby, what do you know about Sean?"

Everything that matters, I think to myself. Out loud, I say, "Not much."

"Do you think I should go for him? I know he's older, but he's pretty cute, right?"

Now the towels feel wrong somehow, like they're sucking my skin dry. I don't want to prolong this conversation, but Leah stands there with her hands on her hips as if I owe her something. I never did like that girl.

"I don't think he's interested in high school girls. I mean, he's twenty-three," I say, looking at the wall.

"Yeah, you're probably right. He talks to you a lot more than he talks to me, though. Sometimes I wonder if he even knows I exist." She takes a step toward the door. "I have to go. See you later." She leaves and I can finally breathe.

The little voice inside my head whispers,
He doesn't even know she exists. You see?
He does like you. I smile to myself and
practically skip down the hall to the staff
room, so blinded by glee I almost crash
into someone coming the other way.

"Sorry, Abby. I didn't see you."

I blink and it's Bethany, a volunteer who's
been here for two years. She tucks a stray
piece of dyed black hair behind her ear.

"That's okay. I wasn't looking either."

She smiles. I'd forgotten how pretty she is.
Most of the time, all I see when I look at
her is the hair and the nose ring and her

chipped nail polish. But she has nice green eyes. Like a cat.

"How's school?" she asks.

"It sucks, like always. I can't wait to get out of high school."

Bethany laughs. "I was the same way. University is so much better, though maybe by the end of term I'll think everything there sucks, too."

In the kennels behind us, I can hear a dog beginning to whine. Bethany looks alarmed. "That's Daisy. I put a leash on her ten minutes ago and forgot I was supposed to take her out. I'd better go. Stay strong,

Abby, even if you're still in high school."
She laughs again before turning around
and hurrying toward Daisy's thin howl.

Later, just as I'm leaving for the day, Sean's
voice calls out to me from the office.
"Abby, do you have a minute?"

I find him by the window, leaning against
the glass, his arms folded across his chest.
My stomach flips—not because he's said
or done anything special, but because he's
in a patch of sunshine, smiling at me, his
lean hips at a cocky angle. It's as if he was
born to stand like that, like he knows it's a
mental picture I'll save forever. How is it
that I haven't rushed him and buried my

face in the curve of his neck?

"It's been pretty quiet here today so I thought I'd leave early. Do you want to get something to eat? There's a cool place not far from here. I can be pretty entertaining after I've had some coffee."

I want to jump up and down and fling my arms in the air. Instead, I say, "I was just on my way out."

He straightens up and begins feeling around in his pockets. "We can leave right now if you want. I'll just ask Bethany to lock up." He pulls out a ring of keys. "I'll drive."

I breathe in and out twice before I answer.

"Sure. I could use a coffee." When his back is turned, I cover my face with my hands because I'm not sure if I'm going to cry or laugh or just have a hysterical fit. Whatever's going to happen, I don't want anyone to see.

▬▬▬ ●

We drive through streets with maple trees lining each side. The leaves are red and yellow, circling through the air as cars speed past. When I was small, I would say I liked fall best because that was when the world was getting ready for sleep and everything was warm and dozy and calm.

Sean is nodding to the beat of the song on the radio. The light from the driver's side window is thick, like butterscotch, and it pools around him. He winks at me.

"I'm sure this song is way before your time. We used to listen to it in my best friend's basement while we raided his father's liquor cabinet." He laughs and taps the steering wheel. "Maybe you should forget I told you that."

"Told me what?" I say.

Sean laughs again and pats my knee with his right hand. I stare at my jeans, at the spot he just touched, and wonder if the

skin underneath has turned pink or purple
or some other color. I can't remember the
last time someone touched me. It burns.
And I like it.

We pull over in front of a coffee shop
with no sign, not even a sandwich board
out front. This is the neighborhood where
all the cool people hang out. You know,
the musicians who wear porkpie hats
and old plumber's shirts they bought at
the local thrift store for two dollars. I
sometimes think I want to live here when
I graduate, rent an apartment with a pair
of roommates and sit on the balcony at
night, drinking tequila or tea. I look into
the café's big front window and see girls

with messy ponytails and rumpled jackets, and boys with spotty facial hair and shrunken sweater vests. I wonder if they have a homing instinct, a kind of hipster sonar that lets them find each other, even in coffee shops with no names. I'm not going to fit in. I never do.

Sean smiles at me. "They have good scones."

I swallow hard. Will the people inside think I'm a kid? Sean's sister? A stupid teenager who only got out of braces three months ago? Then I remember. *Be the girl he wants.* I reach for the door handle. "Scones are good," I say and push myself out of the car before I can think anymore.

When we step through the door, no one even looks up and I wonder if it's worse to be seen and judged, or not to be noticed at all. I fidget until Sean points to a table in the corner. "I'll get us some coffee. What would you like?"

"Decaf," I blurt. "Maybe with milk?"

He comes back with two plates, one with a blueberry scone and the other with a sandwich. "I hope you're not one of those freaks who doesn't eat blueberries," he says.

We talk while we eat, and he tells me about the dog he had when he was a kid, a big white Samoyed who would walk

him to school every morning and come back at three fifteen to walk him home. "By the time I got to grade nine, it was a little embarrassing. But he would stand there with this big grin and I couldn't be mad at him. And he looked so happy to be walking home with me, as if that's all he ever wanted out of life."

I feel like saying, *Who could blame him?* But instead I just smile, trying not to remember how my mother used to pick us up from school every afternoon, her arms open as if she hadn't seen us in years. We'd run to her and almost toppled her over, laughing like lunatics.

Maybe he sees the memory in my face because he touches my hand lightly, and the hairs on the back of my neck stand up. "And then my grandfather would meet us in the front yard and hang out with me until my mother came home from work." Sean takes a gulp of his coffee. "Have I ever told you about him? He was the most amazing old guy ever."

Sean's voice falls and then rises, like the ocean on a calm day. I could float on his words, water lapping in the dips and curves of my waist, my neck, my elbow. He tells me that his grandfather used to play the ukulele at a tiki restaurant in New York.

"You know, one of those places with the fake palm trees and coconut drinks," he says as he chews on his sandwich. "I still have that ukulele. I keep it in the closet at home."

"That's so cool. You should bring it to the shelter sometime. I'd love to see it."

Sean looks at me, then looks away. I think I've said something wrong, or revealed that I'm too young or too dumb or too eager. I think I should say something, but the seconds keep passing and, now, anything I say will just break what's become an awkward silence, and that's even more awkward. I pull on a chunk of my hair and look at a row of antique teacups lining a shelf above the counter.

Finally, he speaks. "My place isn't far from here. We could stop by if you want." He fiddles with his mug and frowns into the table.

"Sure. I have some time before I have to go home." I say this with a straight face, but the smile isn't far from the surface. *I am the girl he wants.*

We don't say much in the car on the way to Sean's apartment. I open the window as wide as it will go and breathe in the air that is part frost, part decay, and part evergreen. It's like Christmas is coming early. I breathe out slowly and try not to worry about dinner or what I'm going to say next.

▬▬▬ ●

His apartment is small, a one-bedroom with no balcony, just a big window that looks out on a sparse front yard. Sean walks ahead of me, waving his arm at the space around him.

"This is the living room, but you probably already guessed that. The bedroom's through that door and the bathroom is over there. It's not very big, but it works for me. The only bad thing is I can't have pets." He points to an empty terrarium sitting on the floor. "Although I'm thinking of sneaking in an iguana."

Before I say anything, he pulls the ukulele out of the hall closet. "Here it is," he

says. "See, that's my grandfather's name scratched on the back." He hands it to me. I trace my finger over the lacquered wood, feel the curves in the body. It's warm to the touch. Before I know what he's doing, Sean pulls out a camera and snaps a picture.

He laughs at my startled face. "You looked so cute. I had to do it." He walks over to a small desk in the corner with a laptop open on its surface and fits the camera into a docking station. "I have some pictures of my grandfather playing, too. I spent the summer scanning in my mom's old photographs and made them into a slideshow for her. Take a look."

His grandfather is deeply tanned but other-
wise looks just like Sean—same blond hair,
same lanky posture. I wonder if Sean loves
anything as much as his grandfather loved
that ukulele. Maybe the dogs. Maybe me,
one day. I blush and turn around.

He looks at me with his eyes turned
down—it's the same way he looks at
the puppies and I stop moving and stare
back. And all of a sudden, I think maybe
I shouldn't be here, that if my parents or
sisters knew I had come to this apartment
alone with a man I barely know, they
would tell me I'm an idiot. Because I know
why he's asked me here. I know what he
thinks I want. And I do. I do want it. I

want to know if it's the way those romance novels that my mom reads describe it—tender and loving and beautiful. Or if it's fast and consuming like in the movies.

He puts his arms around my waist and kisses me, his lips soft and light as if he's unsure, too. I step into him and the doubtful voice in my head quickly dies down. I wanted to come here. I made him love me. Whatever we do now is what I asked for.

Now the kiss is hot and liquid and travels down my throat and into the rest of me until it settles between my legs. Before I can stop myself, I gasp out loud. I'm not sure I can stand up much longer. My knees have turned to goo.

"The bedroom," Sean says, taking a step toward it.

I don't reply, but I don't need to because his body and my body are crab-walking together in the same direction. He slides his hand into the small of my back and I've forgotten where we're going, but as long as we're going together, that's all that matters.

━━━ ●

The afternoon light spills into the bedroom from the window. Somehow, I've managed to take off all my clothes and lie on Sean's bed. Everything is in plain sight: the blue duvet cover, the pine dresser in

the corner, and me, naked. I look down at myself and immediately look away. I look like an abandoned mannequin—pale and motionless, my legs stuck straight out at an angle that isn't quite human. I don't want him to see me like this, but it's too late. He lies beside me. His body is long and smooth and golden, and I forget that I'm nervous. He kisses me again and I slide closer.

My nerve endings snap to attention when he touches me, as if from little shocks. Then his fingers run down my left side to my hip and it feels like I'm lying in a warm bath, a place where I can forget about the time or how lonely it is at school. I close

my eyes and breathe out. He kisses me on the shoulder, on my breasts, between my thighs. *Yes, this*, I think. *This is what I want.*

"You'll have to move a bit," Sean says. I open my eyes and he's hovering above me, balancing on his elbows. I must look confused because he sighs quietly and says, "Just your legs. This way." I do what he says and I'm embarrassed. I should know what to do without him telling me. But where would I have learned that?

Even though he lies on top of me now, I'm suddenly cold and covered with goose bumps. I know what's supposed to happen. This is the moment before we're going to

have sex. I will no longer be that girl who dreams about love and romance. Instead, I'll be the girl who is living it.

But I'm scared. I didn't plan on being scared.

Maybe he knows, because he whispers to me, "Don't worry. I have a condom."

At first, it doesn't hurt, it just feels funny and new. *Silly*, I think to myself. *There's nothing to worry about*. But then, it's like I'm splitting in two, like I'm a paper doll slowly being ripped in half. I don't scream or cry; instead, I bite my lip and push my fists into the mattress as if I could punch my way out of this. All I can hear is Sean's

breathing. He doesn't know it hurts. He hasn't stopped.

I try to remember how it felt when he was kissing me. But the memory is gone and I'm left with this rhythmic pain and the sound of his skin slapping against mine.

Finally, he's finished. He rolls over and smiles at me, as if this was something I should have enjoyed. I don't know what to do next, so I turn my head away and look out the window. I can see the apartment building across the street. Someone on the top floor has left the window open and a white curtain billows out into the wind, ballooning and collapsing. I want to get up,

but I don't want to be the first one to move.

"I'll just be in the bathroom for a minute," he says. As he gets up and walks away, I look at his body, still long and beautiful, not the sort of body I would ever think could make me hurt like that. Maybe we can talk about it later. Maybe next time will be better. Or maybe I should end this now, because I can't imagine wanting to be in his bed ever again.

I stand up and pull on my sweatshirt. I'm not sure where my other clothes are, so I walk into the living room, blinking as I step past the big front window. His laptop is on, the picture of his grandfather still

open. I reach out and tap the mouse pad until another gallery appears, and I search for the photo of me with the ukulele. I squint at the thumbnail-sized images and click on one that seems familiar. I look at myself, hair falling in my face, my fingers on the frets as if I know what I'm doing. I smile, then touch the mouse pad again. For a second, I'm not sure what I'm looking at. It's a picture of me, standing outside the shelter with one of the dogs, waiting for the walk signal at the crosswalk. I've never seen this photo. I didn't even know he took it.

I look annoyed and hurried, my forehead wrinkled with concentration. He must

have been standing right by the front door. How could I not have noticed him when I've been spending most of my shifts tracking his every move? On its own, the image means nothing, but, here, on Sean's computer, it means so much more—there I am, completely unaware of what he's doing or thinking or even where he is. He let me pursue him. He watched me make a fool of myself whenever I spoke to him. He must have had a plan, too.

This is all wrong. Or maybe it isn't. Maybe he's always liked me and was waiting for the right time. Maybe the photograph was just a lucky moment when he had a camera and I happened to be standing

there. There has to be a perfectly reasonable explanation. I'm sure of it.

I touch the mouse pad, half sick at the possibility there might be more. I rub my eyes with the back of my hand and blink to clear my vision. As the blurriness lifts, I see another photograph, but it isn't of me. This girl has curly hair and freckles and is posing in front of his car. I click again. Another girl, this one sitting at a table in the same café we just went to, a closed-mouth, glossy pink smile on her face. I tap the mouse pad one more time. I see Bethany, the pretty, nose-ringed girl at the shelter, her dyed black hair over one eye. She sits on a couch, an empty terrarium

on the floor beside her. It's this apartment. This very room.

I take a step back and look at the ceiling to avoid seeing those pictures again. I know he's not my boyfriend, and I don't think this one afternoon means he's never had sex with a girl before. But those pictures aren't old. Bethany looks the same as she did when I saw her two hours ago. Even the light in the café looks the same. I look down at the terrarium, still empty, still in the same spot.

This whole thing had been engineered by Sean. He thought about it, planned every question he ever asked me, and practiced

looking like he cared about the answers.
He wanted me, sure, but it wasn't just me.
I wasn't *the* girl. I was just *a* girl. The walls
in this room know everything—they've
seen everything, watched him kiss Bethany
and me and every other girl whose name I
don't know. I scratch at my arm. I feel like
I'm covered in something sticky and gross.

I hear the bathroom door slam shut.
I know without looking that Sean is
standing over my shoulder, that he sees
what I'm staring at. Now we both know.

I turn around—his face is fallen and
empty, like a three-day-old balloon. I can't
tell what he's thinking, or what he might

say. There's no point in waiting, so I walk
past him and pick up my jeans and socks
and shoes, then run to the bedroom to
get my underwear. I can't stay another
second in this apartment, or look again at
his expressionless, stupidly silent face. I've
never dressed so quickly in my life and,
still, I think I should go faster. On my way
through the living room, Sean puts a hand
on my arm.

"Stop," he says quietly. "I want you to stay."

But it's as if he hasn't touched me, and I
rush past him, my eyes on my backpack
and then on the door to the hallway. I run
down the three flights of stairs and out

through the fire exit onto the footpath. I
don't remember what streets we took to
get here, so I run west, toward the setting
sun. I don't look back until I'm a block and
a half away and can't tell which building
is his anymore. *Thank God*, I think. I don't
stop running.

▬ ●

I don't know where I'm going, only that
these sidewalks have to lead someplace
I recognize. Rush hour is over and
the streets are quiet, so no one notices
my stumbling feet or hears my jagged
breathing. It's starting to feel chilly, but

my head is pounding and hot. I run into
a small city park and straight into a bed
of rhododendrons. I throw up, and for the
first time today, I feel like this is the very
thing I'm supposed to be doing.

I sit down on a bench and search my
pockets and backpack for change. Nothing.
I don't have enough money for bus fare,
not even a quarter to call home. If I could,
I would go back in time to those nights
when I'd fall asleep with my head in my
mother's lap as she told the same story
about the emperor's new clothes. "But
there really were no clothes and everyone
could see he was naked, right down to his
rump." And I would giggle as if I'd never

heard her say it before. Then, she would stroke my hair until I drifted off, her hand warm and dry.

That was a long time ago. Before my dad had to work two jobs to pay the rent on our house. Before my mom started hating us and hanging out with the younger women from her work. Before I thought I could turn our family into what it used to be by wiping every spill and cooking every night. I wish I could go home right now and curl up with my mother and listen to the sound of my father snoring in the big recliner by the fireplace. But I know that my parents aren't home and that Liz is hungry and grumpy and Chelsea

is struggling to cook dinner. No one will stroke my hair or warm my feet in her hands. So I may as well stay here for a while, where I can hug myself and the only people who'll see me are strangers. I can say out loud to the tree beside me, *I didn't know*, and no one will understand what I'm talking about. And then, I can cry.

•